In the City of Dreams

A Magical World Awaits You
Read

THE
SECRETS
OF
DROON

THE SECRETS OF DROON

— TONY ABBOTT —

In the City of Dreams

Illustrated by Royce Fitzgerald
Cover illustration by Tim Jessell

SCHOLASTIC INC.
New York Toronto London Auckland Sydney
Mexico City New Delhi Hong Kong Buenos Aires

For Droonlings everywhere

For more information about the continuing saga of Droon,
please visit Tony Abbott's website at
www.tonyabbottbooks.com

ISBN-13: 978-0-545-09881-6
ISBN-10: 0-545-09881-5

12   11   10 9 8 7 6 5 4 3 2   9   10   11   12   13   14/0

Printed in the U.S.A.
First printing, February 2009

Contents

One

Secrets and . . . Fibs!

"Eric Hinkle?"

Mrs. Michaels peered down from the auditorium stage at the students sitting in the front row. "Eric, are you there?"

No answer.

"Where in the world is Eric?" Mrs. Michaels asked her students.

While her classmates turned and looked around at one another, Julie Rubin whispered to her friend Neal Kroger,

"That's just the problem, isn't it? Eric isn't in *this* world at all!"

It was true. Eric wasn't in this world.

For the past three days he had been far away in the mysterious land of Droon.

Droon was the secret world the kids had discovered under Eric's basement. It was a marvelous land of fantastic creatures, adventure, and magic, both good and bad.

Eric had fallen to bad magic.

"Can someone run back to the classroom and see if Eric is there?" asked Mrs. Michaels.

Julie raised her hand eagerly. "I'll go!"

"Me, too!" said Neal. "We'll also check the cafeteria. Eric might be sneaking crackers from the kitchen closet . . . or wherever they hide them."

"Thank you," said the teacher. "We need to start rehearsing this play."

As Julie and Neal hustled out to the hall, they recalled the frightening events of three days before. The friends had been far in the snowy north of Droon, when Eric was wounded by an ice dagger aimed at the wizard Galen Longbeard.

Hurled by one of Emperor Ko's fiendish Nesh warriors, the ice dagger carried a dangerous poison intended to fulfill a prophecy — to strike down one of the sons of Zara: Galen, Lord Sparr, or Urik.

While Galen and Sparr had been present, the man thought to be Urik had turned out to be the mysterious Prince of Stars. But that didn't matter, because when the poisoned dagger was thrown, Eric thought only of protecting the wizards.

He threw himself in the way.

Galen was saved, but Eric was hit.

Within seconds, he grew icy cold and slipped into unconsciousness.

Galen hurried Julie and Neal home to the Upper World, then rushed Eric to Jaffa City to try to reverse Ko's dark magic.

That was three very long days ago.

Neal and Julie had heard nothing since.

"I can't understand why Keeah doesn't call us to Droon," said Neal grimly as they walked down the empty hall. "We need to see our friend. But we've had no dreams of Droon. And the magic soccer ball hasn't given us any messages. Should we be worried? I mean . . . really worried?"

Julie frowned. "I don't want to think about it. Worrying about Eric isn't going to help him. Besides, we've got enough to worry about here at home. Every time I pretend to be Eric, I feel like I'm lying. Being him — and me — for the last three days is more than I can handle. Our poor parents don't even know!"

"At least you can change shape," said Neal. "That scratch you got from a wing-wolf lets you transform into anyone —"

Julie gave Neal a sharp look. "I'm pretty sure your genie magic lets you do the same. Why am I the one who always has to change?"

"Because Eric and I are always together," said Neal. "It would be weird if Eric hung out with you. No offense."

"Let's just do it," Julie grumbled.

Checking first that no one was watching, Julie twirled on one foot. When she stopped, she looked just like Eric.

"I wish you really were him," said Neal.

"I know," said Julie. "Come on. Let's go back and do our best."

The two friends, now looking like Eric and Neal, reentered the auditorium and took the stage.

"Good, you're here," said Mrs. Michaels.

"Now, Eric, let's rehearse your scene with Neal. Page one. Ready? Begin."

And the two friends began to run lines.

As difficult as it was for Julie and Neal to pretend that Eric was with them, it was harder still being unable to get to Droon to see their friend.

Every afternoon after school, they had tramped down to his basement closet. They'd closed the door behind them. They'd switched off the light. And they'd waited.

The staircase to Droon had not appeared.

Each day, the two friends woke up more worried than the day before. Each day, they went to sleep not knowing.

Then it happened.

Just as they were finishing up the first scene of the play, Neal turned to Julie and said, "I think I see the moon —"

And something round and white dropped straight from the ceiling.

Whump! It struck Neal on the head.

"Owww!" he cried, falling to his knees.

Whump! It hit him again, and he fell forward onto his hands.

Whump! It smacked him a third time, and he dropped facedown onto the floor.

"Neal, are you all right?" called Mrs. Michaels, running over.

"I guess," grumbled Neal. Then he saw what had struck him on the head.

It was not the moon.

It was a soccer ball.

Neal gasped. ***Julie!*** he said silently. ***The soccer ball. It's our magic soccer ball!***

Two hastily scribbled words suddenly seemed to float across the surface of the ball.

Ylkciuq Emoc.

They were the words, written backward, that both friends had been hoping for every moment of the last three days.

Ylkciuq emoc meant *Come quickly*.

Hooray! Julie said silently, looking at Neal. **We're going to Droon!**

Mrs. Michaels helped Neal to his feet. "Everyone take a break while I try to figure out how that soccer ball got up there!"

"You bet!" said Julie, in Eric's voice. "We'll be outside, running our lines."

"Or just plain running," Neal whispered, scooping up the soccer ball.

Five minutes later, the two friends were dashing through backyards, across driveways, and straight up the sidewalk to Eric's house.

Without being seen, the two friends slipped quietly through the side door and flew down the basement stairs. By the time

Neal had safely stowed away the soccer ball, Julie had changed back into herself.

"We've never actually gone to Droon without Eric before," said Julie, entering the closet under the stairs and reaching for the ceiling light. "It's weird, you know?"

Neal nodded. "Let's hope this is the first and only time."

"And that Eric comes safely back with us," said Julie. She tugged the chain on the light — *click!* — and the bulb went dark.

All at once — *whoosh!* — the floor of the closet vanished. In its place was the top step of a long, curving staircase. The wispy pink clouds of Droon's sky swirled below.

"Eric, here we come!" said Julie as the two friends ran down the stairs together.

The moment they pushed past the clouds, they spied the familiar towers of Jaffa City.

But the closer they came, the more changes they noticed to the jaunty, springtime capital.

Gloomy pennants were draped on the city walls. Black flags flew atop the towers. And inside the gates, throngs of somber-clothed citizens streamed toward the royal palace.

"Oh, no," said Neal. "Oh, no."

Rushing down the stairs, the two friends hurried to join the crowd. Julie stopped a woman dressed in black, who was hobbling toward the palace. "Tell us, how is Eric Hinkle?"

The woman raised her eyes. They were moist. She tried to speak, then cupped her hand over her mouth and hid her face.

The two friends shared a frightened look.

"Come on!" said Neal, grabbing Julie's hand. "We can't waste a second!"

Two

Room of Gloom

Julie and Neal hurried up the palace steps.

"Eric is in the royal bedchamber," said the first guard they passed.

"Please go quickly!" said the second.

The two friends raced through one glittering hall after another, from staircase to golden staircase, all the way to the uppermost room.

They stopped in surprise when they

reached the hall outside the royal chamber. It was crowded with many old friends.

Pacing back and forth in front of the door was Shago, the whiskered master thief whose skills had often helped them on their journeys. He smiled sadly when he saw the friends.

"To see you again like this," Shago said, sniffling. "Eric is so weak. . . ."

"But he will rally once he senses you are here!" said Khan, king of the Lumpies. His boots were dusty from his journey from the distant desert of Lumpland.

"Everyone, stand aside!" said Queen Ortha while Batamogi, the Oobja king, waved the way clear for Neal and Julie to enter the room. Ortha, ruler of the clever Bangledorn monkeys, bowed as the children passed. Batamogi did the same. Like the others, both showed signs of long and weary travel.

The chamber itself was crowded but nearly silent, except for the continuous murmur of a low voice in the corner.

The sorcerer, Lord Sparr, blind and old before his time, sat rocking back and forth on a small stool, whispering to himself. His tattered cloak was draped low over his face, obscuring all but his thin gray beard. His hands were locked together atop a rusty saber that he used as a cane.

Crowded nearest to the bed were Galen; Max, the spider troll; the royal couple, King Zello and Queen Relna; and Princess Keeah.

Eric himself was lying motionless in an ornate four-poster bed, his face as pale as the midday moon, his slight body barely showing beneath the heavy blankets.

"Oh . . ." Julie gasped.

Keeah rose to greet her friends. Her eyes were red from crying.

"Dear friends," she said, hugging them. "I'm glad you've come. Expeditions have been sent all over Droon to find a cure for Eric's dark wound."

"But none has been found," said Max.

"We hope that Eric senses you are here," said Relna, "and this will help him heal."

"Hope!" said Galen, storming from one end of the chamber to the other. "In my youth, I could move stars. I fought armies single-handed. I braved dangers unknown! But I cannot help a little boy. Eric is like a son to me. A grandson. An old friend. A brother! And yet . . ."

"Even Sparr cannot help," said Zello, gesturing to the sorcerer, still rocking on his stool. "Since Eric was struck, he has been in a dark world of his own."

"Yet we cannot give up hope," said Max. "We must never give up hope."

"Never," said Galen, turning to a large, elaborately framed mirror and studying it closely. The children knew it was a magic mirror through which the wizard could see all of Droon.

"No rock, no pebble, no grain of dust shall remain unturned in our quest to find a cure for this terrible wound!" the wizard said.

Keeah put her hand on Eric's forehead.

"So pale, so cold!" she said, pulling another blanket to his chin. "It's as if Eric's spirit has left him and gone far away. If we only knew where his spirit has gone!"

Where my spirit has gone!

Eric's eyelids felt as heavy as lead. He struggled to open them. When he finally succeeded, he saw a room filled with people. There were his friends from home, Julie and Neal. And there were Galen and

Max and Queen Relna and Khan, the pillow king.

"Hi, everyone!" he said. But his words sounded strange and far away, as if someone else had said them. "What's up?"

His friends all looked down at the bed, though none answered him. Their expressions were . . . what? Sad? Worried?

Why? he wondered.

And here was Keeah, bending to him, her fingers extended to touch his forehead. She pulled them away. Strange. He hadn't felt her hand on his skin.

Instinctively, he reached for the bandage on his shoulder. The wound under it was open, raw, and unhealed. He remembered that.

And yet . . . the wound didn't hurt.

With great effort, Eric propped himself up in the large bed, pushed the blankets aside, and slid down to the floor.

"I feel pretty good for someone who's supposedly injured," he said.

All the sad faces were still looking down at the bed. He followed their gaze.

He shuddered.

On the bed he saw — himself!

"What?" he said. "But I'm over here!"

His face — *his* face — was as white as the pillow behind it. His hair was damp and matted, as if wet cloths had been applied to his forehead. His eyeglasses were placed lovingly on the side table next to a goblet of water.

Eric touched his own face. His glasses were right there atop his nose. How could that be?

"How could I still be in the bed? Am I asleep? Am I dreaming? Hey! Anyone?"

No one spoke.

Then, all at once, something strange happened.

The air . . . *rippled* . . . across the room like a wave. It seemed to come from the big mirror. It flowed past him and settled on the boy in the bed.

His pale white face grew paler still!

"This is so weird!" Eric said. "Hey! People!"

It was then that he realized something else. When that ripple had passed over, the people standing by the bed looked both sadder and strangely different. Eric found himself struggling to recall the names he had just had in mind.

That boy with blond hair was a friend, right? And the girl in the red T-shirt. He knew her, for sure. The tall wizard . . . his name began with a *G* or something. And the pretty blond girl with the crown and the wet eyes — she was a princess . . . wasn't she?

Eric stepped over to the mirror. At first he saw only mist. Looking more closely, he began to make out tall buildings and domes, canals and bridges, and streets paved with stones of different colors. A city?

A wild city!

In the center of the streets stood a large palace of colorful stones. It had curving walls and steps circling up the highest tower.

"What is that place?" he asked.

You know its name. . . .

Eric spun around to see a dark-cloaked man seated on a stool. The man's head rose slowly to reveal eyes that flashed under his hood.

"You heard me?" asked Eric. "But . . . who are you?"

The man's lips did not move, but his words sounded in Eric's head.

The city's name is Saaa . . .

And the name of the wild city came to Eric.

"Saaa . . ." he said to himself.

There was a sudden commotion at the chamber door. Shago and Khan jumped aside as Ortha called out, "Make way, everyone! Pasha comes!"

The crowd parted, and Pasha, the diminutive carpet weaver with the striped cap and long mustache, scampered into the room, cradling a small green bird in his hands.

"Friends!" he panted. "Since Lord Sparr's blindness, I have cared for his little bird, Isha. Now Isha brings word of a miraculous cure from the very fringes of the Dark Lands —"

"And look here!" said Galen suddenly, staring into the magic mirror. "The image clears. I see a city of bridges, water, domes, and streets of many colors —"

"Eric is moving!" cried Keeah as Eric twitched suddenly and his lips parted.

"Isha has described a magical city in the east," Pasha went on. "A city of wonder."

"I know this distant place!" said Galen, staring at the mirror's image. "It is —"

"The city of . . ." Pasha continued.

The moment Pasha and Galen spoke the name together, Eric sat straight up in bed and shouted at the top of his lungs —

"Samarindo!"

Then, as if the effort to speak was more than he could bear, Eric sank back into the sheets, his breathing slowed, and he grew even paler than before.

"The cure will be found in Samarindo!" cried Galen. "Samarindo, city of magic! City of danger! Keeah, you must go at once!"

Three

To the Carpet!

Princess Keeah rushed to the door. "City of danger? I don't care about danger. I'm going there now! Julie, Neal, come with me —"

"Wait!" said Max. "In the mirror!"

The moment the children looked in the mirror, they saw the air tremble away from the city's palace like water from a pebble dropped in a pond. The ripple spread from street to street, and the long, broad avenues leading from the palace changed their direction like writhing worms.

"Legends call Samarindo the City of Dreams," said Galen. "Now you see why."

A bridge arched here; a river snaked there. Buildings vanished for a moment before re-forming, altered, somewhere else. Paved plazas with fountains became bare clearings, hills became valleys, streams crossed by bridges became streets, twisted and crabbed.

And through it all, the colorful palace in the center of the city did not move. But its colors dimmed a little, fading so they appeared almost gray.

"Legends say the city's ruler wears a Dream Crown," said Galen. "The crown is the source of this powerful magic."

"But the City of Dreams is a city of nightmares for anyone looking for something," said Julie. "How will we find the cure?"

"Lord Sparr will not mind if I offer little Isha as your guide," said Pasha, petting the bird. "Dreams or not, her sense of direction is first-rate. She'll help you find the cure."

Keeah looked at Sparr, rocking and whispering to himself, then turned back to Pasha. "If you come, too," she said.

The little rug weaver beamed. "Me? Really? A mission? Do you mean it?"

"We do," said the princess.

"Then I'd be honored!" he said, bowing so low that his nose touched the ground. "Now I can test my latest carpet innovation, invisibility threads. I've made a completely undetectable flying carpet!"

"Great! Let's go get it," said Neal.

"It's already here!" said Pasha. He tugged at the air next to him and — *floop!* — a carpet suddenly appeared.

"The crew is set!" said Galen. "Keeah —"

"Not yet!" said a sudden voice.

All eyes turned to the corner.

Lord Sparr raised his head to Keeah. His cheeks — nearly as pale as Eric's — were glistening with tears. "Keeah, know one thing. While you seek the cure my little Isha has found, I will not leave Eric's side, no matter where he goes."

"Where he goes?" Keeah said. "But —"

"Remember!" he said. Then, patting Isha's head, he lowered his own until his aged face could not be seen. He resumed rocking back and forth on the stool.

"Thank you, Lord Sparr," Keeah said.

Galen had watched his brother silently. "We all thank you. Now, Keeah, take this."

He handed her a mirror that looked like a perfect miniature of the larger one.

"It will help us keep in touch. In the meantime, Max and I will consult the ancient books for other possible cures."

"Khan, Shago, and I will sail to the far-away island of Mikos," said Zello, "in hopes a cure may lie hidden in Bazra's treasure fortress. Ortha, Batamogi, and the others, please search the distant reaches of the Saladian Plains."

"We will," said Batamogi, bowing.

Queen Relna took her daughter's hand. "Sparr and I will look after Eric. While he is in danger, we're all in danger."

Keeah nodded, wiping away a tear. She took one last look at Eric, paler than ever, then turned and joined her friends at the window.

Moments later, she, Julie, and Neal, with Pasha as pilot, flew the carpet — visible for the moment — out of the room and across the rooftops of Jaffa City. There was a chorus of cheers from the towns-people below as they swept by.

After conversing quietly with Isha, the carpet weaver set a course southeast, toward the Dark Lands.

Though the air over Jaffa City was sunny, the sky grew increasingly overcast and chilly the farther they flew into enemy territory.

"I'll never forget when I first heard of Samarindo," said Neal.

Everyone knew what he meant.

Samarindo was home to two princesses the children had met once before. Their names were Looma and Sarla, and they were violently attracted to Neal's wavy blond hair.

"I've decided to keep my turban pulled safely low," he said. "Of course, it's hard to blame the girls. I do have awe-some hair —"

All at once, Isha fluttered up and began to tweet noisily.

"We are?" said the little weaver. He peered over the edge of the rug. "So we are! Look, everyone. There it is!"

And there it was.

A walled city of domes and bridges and streets and towers appeared amid a vast desert of purple sand dunes stretching all the way to the Dark Lands in the east.

"It actually looks beautiful," said Julie.

"The next dream will change it, no doubt," said Keeah. "Pasha, let's land just inside the wall."

"Aye-aye," the little pilot said. He gently landed the rug in a narrow alley beneath the city wall, folded the carpet to the size of a handkerchief, and stowed it under his cap.

The sounds of a busy city bubbled around them. Voices called, pilka hooves

clopped on the cobblestones, and the melodic strains of strange instruments filled the air.

"Cool," said Neal. "Now where?"

"Isha will tell us," said Pasha, listening closely to the bird's tweets and whistles. "She says the cure can be found at . . . the Silver Dome. Isha, where is the Silver Dome?"

Twittering once, the bird dipped to the end of the alley, looked both ways, and flew left.

"Left it is!" said Keeah. "Let's follow!"

The four friends hurried after the little bird and entered a street where dozens of shops bustled with life and the air sang with voices. Creatures of every sort milled about the streets. Some were small and scaly, others plump and furry. The children decided not to attract attention but to simply follow Isha as she swooped from street to street.

Entering one narrow alley, they spied a low-roofed shop piled high with brass urns, lamps, and pots, while another featured scarves of every hue and size.

"Samarindo *is* lovely," Keeah said as she breathed in the warm morning air. It was scented with the fragrance of summer flowers. "But Isha is flying so quickly, we can't pause."

Neal stopped in his tracks. "Except to eat!"

He pointed to a tiny pie shop squeezed between a bucket stand and a shop filled with curly-tipped shoes. Neal spied a little creature in the window of the pie shop. It had knobby blue skin, wild whiskers, and one eye in the center of its forehead that brightened when it saw Neal.

"Yes?" said the creature.

"Blueberry, please —" Neal began.

All of a sudden, the ground quivered as if a giant wave were washing over the street.

"Brace yourselves. It's a dream!" said Julie.

Pasha grabbed Neal and pulled him back, while the shopkeepers quickly grabbed their wares and held them steady.

"Here's my card!" said the pie maker, stuffing a card into Neal's hand even as the shop began to fade. "But the address . . . is . . . wrong!"

In less time than it takes to say it, the street buckled and sank and changed. When the dream finally passed, Neal was flat on the ground without his turban, Julie and Keeah were twisted in a knot, and Pasha was on his knees, gently cradling Isha in his hands.

Instead of a lively cobblestone street, they found themselves in a bare, open square paved with ashes.

The air had darkened.

Clouds had drifted overhead.

And the place where the pie shop had been was now occupied by two orange-haired young princesses, one dressed all in pink, the other in green.

They spied Neal and screamed.

"My goodness, it's him!" cried the one named Sarla.

"And he brought his hair with him!" yelled the one named Looma.

Neal shrieked, "The instant I'm not wearing my turban, you show up!"

"Get him!" the girls cried together.

"Girls, halt!" snapped Keeah, shooting violet sparks from her fingertips. "Now!"

The two princesses froze.

"Don't hurt us," pleaded Looma.

"I won't," said Keeah. "But please don't bother Neal or his hair. We've come to Samarindo seeking a cure for our sick friend. We can't waste time running away from you."

The sisters looked at each other, at Neal's hair, and at Keeah's sparking fingers, then sighed.

"Fine," said Sarla, the one dressed in pink. "It hardly matters, anyway. Nothing's fun anymore. Not since . . . Tuesday."

"Tuesday?" said Pasha, counting on his fingers. "Tuesday is exactly when Isha flew from Jaffa City to find a cure. She found it here."

Looma, the one in the green gown, nodded. "It's also the day the Dream Crown was stolen and the city became strange and frightening."

"Galen told us about the crown," said Julie.

"It belongs to our father, Boola, duke of Samarindo," said Sarla. "The dreams from his Dream Crown are why people have come here for years. Father would dream of wonderful things, and they would happen! He's always used the crown for good."

"And for fun," added Looma. "Food appeared when we were hungry. Rain came to help flowers grow. On the first day of summer, my father dreamed up a beach right in the center of town. It was lovely."

"Only now it's a terrible place," said Looma. "Since that *thing* stole his crown."

"What thing?" said Keeah.

"Like a big wolf," said Sarla. "With wings."

The children looked at one another.

Julie's eyes widened. "You mean . . . a wingwolf?"

"That's it!" both princesses said together.

Wingwolves were beasts from the ancient past. The kids had encountered them before, when the wingwolves were working for Ko. A wingwolf's scratch had given Julie the ability to fly and to change shape.

"Not to mention the flock of hideous fire dragons!" said Looma. "But they're all just working for someone else who's taken over our father's palace and his crown."

"Wingwolves and fire dragons and stolen crowns," said Neal. "Samarindo is in trouble."

Keeah paced back and forth, then stopped. "We'd like to help your father get his crown back and stop your city's bad dreams. But first we have to find a place called the Silver Dome. That's where the cure can be found."

"And I fear Isha, our guide, is getting confused by all the dreams," said Pasha.

"Well, here comes another one!" said Looma. "The palace is shaking again. Everyone hold on to something —"

"Not my hair!" said Neal, jumping away from the princesses.

As the friends huddled close together, the sun dimmed. The sky turned gray. The ash-paved square vanished into a downward-curving street with torches along the walls.

The giggle twins were nowhere in sight.

And neither was Isha!

"Isha?" said Pasha. "Where is Isha? Isha! Oh, dear, now we're really lost!"

"Lost? You're not lost," growled a deep voice. "Because *I* found you!"

The four friends looked up.

Crouched on a nearby rooftop was a

tall, wolflike creature with purple-red fur. From his back arched a pair of dark wings.

Julie gasped. "A wingwolf!"

"Captain Talon, to be exact," said the wolf. "But you got it wrong, miss. Not *a* wingwolf, *ten* wingwolves! I say, boys, that's your cue."

There came a loud fluttering of wings, and the roof crowded with nearly a dozen wolfish beasts. They slashed the air with their claws.

"Guys," said Keeah, "we should run —"

But before the friends could move, Captain Talon shouted, "Attack!"

Four

Streets of Water

Eric Hinkle saw his own pale figure sit up and shout, "Samarindo!" then fall back again. But he was more interested in the magic mirror's vision of the city.

He watched the air ripple down one cobblestone street after another, reach right through the mirror, and wash over him.

"It tingles!" he said. "Cool!"

He felt an urge to touch the mirror. He did. His fingers slid right into the image as if into water. He felt another urge — to step into the mirror. He did that, too.

He slipped right into the mirror. Instantly, the royal bedchamber and the crowd of people around him disappeared. He stepped down and felt a cobblestone beneath his foot. All around him, the air jangled with the sound of bells and the babble of many voices.

"This is so unbelievably cool!" he said. "I'm in Samarindo! I love it!"

Then he saw a pie shop and felt hungry. But when he approached, he realized he couldn't see his reflection in the shop window.

"Weird window," he said, knocking on it. But his knock sounded more like a light tap. Eric looked at his fist and frowned.

"Hello?" said a voice from the shop. A

creature with bumpy blue skin looked out the door with one big eye.

"Hello," said Eric. "I don't know how I came here, but I'm really hungry and —"

"No one!" said the blue creature. "If only that blond boy had bought a pie!"

Eric frowned. "But excuse me —"

The little creature disappeared into the shop and slammed the door behind it.

"Fine. Be that way," Eric grumbled. "I don't want your pie, anyway!"

Stepping down the street once more, Eric saw an odd, wing-shaped shadow move across the cobblestones ahead of him. But when he looked up, there was nothing there.

"Weird and a half," he said to himself. "But so is everything else here."

At first, he simply wandered down the streets of Samarindo, enjoying the strange and wondrous sights of the city. But soon he found that he was actually following the wing-shaped shadow. From street to street, from alley to bridge to square, he felt drawn by the shadow. No matter how quickly or slowly he walked, the shadow floated at the same pace.

At last he heard the sound of flowing water. "A river?" he said. He closed his eyes, and the image of a boat popped into his mind.

"Of course! The shadow's leading me to the water to find a boat. I need a boat!"

Eric walked faster until he turned down a street that dipped to a low wall.

The shadow slipped past the wall to the other side. Eric leaned over and saw a small wooden boat moored to the riverbank. Resting on its seat was a single oar.

"And there's my boat!" he exclaimed.

The shadow moved down the river.

"Wait for me!" said Eric. He climbed into the boat. It barely made a splash when he sat down. He tried to loosen the rope that held the boat to the bank, but he found he couldn't. In fact, Eric realized, he could barely see his hands.

"I have to follow the shadow! Come on!" he said, frustrated.

Finally, he managed to untie the rope. The boat began to drift down the river.

After several tries, Eric was able to slide the oar from the seat and lower it into the water. He managed to row once, then twice, and the boat glided more swiftly down the canal.

Rounding a bend in the river, Eric heard a tweeting noise. He saw a green bird fly overhead. It sped away.

Turning around another bend, Eric spied some winged creatures with wolf heads chasing a bunch of children and a little man with a long striped cap.

Eric didn't stop rowing. "I can't get involved. I don't even know them."

Strangely, as soon as he left the children behind, he found that every stroke of the oar became easier, and the boat glided along swiftly.

As he drifted around a third bend in the river, he saw what looked like the face of a boy his age floating in midair.

When the boy saw Eric, his eyes bugged out, his mouth opened, and he screamed at the top of his lungs. "A ghost!"

"Same to you," murmured Eric.

And he rowed on.

Blam! Blam!

Keeah blasted violet sparks as she, Julie, Neal, and Pasha tried desperately to escape Captain Talon and his band of flying

creatures. But the wingwolves dodged her sparks and took up the chase, driving them deep into the streets.

The friends raced down long alleys and shot around corner after corner until they spied a ramshackle old pilka stable.

They dived inside and hid.

For minutes, they listened, unmoving.

"Maybe they didn't see us," whispered Pasha. "Perhaps they flew on."

"They're out there," said Neal. "They'll pick us off the second we try to leave."

"I don't get what wingwolves are doing here in the first place," said Julie. "They're ancient beings with ties to Ko and Gethwing. But Ko fell down a bottomless pit, and Gethwing's still trapped in the Underworld."

"These are not standard wingwolves," said Pasha. "I knew there was something strange about Captain Talon's way of talking. Their purple-red fur convinced me. They're eastern wingwolves! Eastern!"

Everyone stared at Pasha.

"And . . ." said Keeah.

"*And,*" said Pasha, "eastern wingwolves are frightened of water, never go near it! We saw a river in Galen's mirror. If dreams haven't changed it yet, we can escape to the river and continue our search for the Silver Dome."

"Okay," said Julie. "But we don't want to wander the streets if the wingwolves are still out there."

The carpet weaver smiled. "Perhaps one of us could hide under my invisible carpet, find the river, and return to help us escape."

The friends looked at one another.

"If we don't hurry," said Keeah, "a new dream may throw us out in the open even farther from the river. I'll go."

"No," said Neal. "I'll go. You check the mirror and see if anything's happened since we left Jaffa City. I'll be back soon."

He threw the carpet over his shoulders and tugged on the fringes. *Blink!*

The rug — with Neal under it — vanished.

"I like you better this way," said Julie.

"Really?" said Neal.

"I'm kidding!" she said. "Hurry before another dream changes everything."

Creeping outside, Neal saw Captain Talon ordering his wolves all around the stable. They didn't see him. Sniffing deeply, he sensed the river close by.

"And I go!" he said to himself. He scrambled invisibly, street after street, until he saw water glinting in the torchlight.

"And I find it!" he said.

As he paused to catch his breath, he saw something drift upriver into view.

It was a small, empty boat.

"Hey, I wonder if we can use that," he said. Lowering the carpet from his face, he peered closely at the boat.

And his eyes bugged out.

The boat was clearly empty, but Neal saw its oar splash in and out of the water as if it were being rowed by . . . by . . .

"A ghost!" he screamed.

The floating face screamed at Eric as he passed, but he didn't stop.

"I have to follow the shadow," he said to himself, "even if I don't know where it's leading me."

With each stroke he seemed to gather strength. He kept the shadow always in sight.

At last, the shadow moved up the bank to a large stone building.

The building was the colorful one he

had seen before, but now it was the color of slate.

Eric was soon at the bank and out of the boat. Back on foot, he followed the shadow to a set of giant doors.

Eric set his hands on two giant doorknobs, but the knobs did not move. He tried again until air rippled out of the building over him, and the knobs began to turn.

"Holy cow!" a voice shouted behind him. "Eric? Eric Hinkle? Hey, Eric —"

"Oh, no," Eric muttered. "That floating head again." He didn't bother turning around.

"Eric, is that you?" said the voice, growing closer. "You look like a ghost! How did you get here all the way from Jaffa City? Did Galen bring you? Turn around. It's Neal —"

"Neal, schmeal!" Eric said, turning on

his heel to face the boy he had seen earlier. "This'll teach you to talk to strangers!"

His hand went up, and silver sparks sprayed the cobblestones at the boy's feet.

"Whoaaaa!" the boy yelled, tumbling head over heels away from the palace.

Eric gripped the knobs once more and turned them as hard as he could. *Click.* Pushing with all his might, he swung the doors open wide.

Torches on both sides of the entrance flickered onto a narrow hallway. The doors shut behind him with a resounding *boom*.

"Enter . . ."

The word was no more than a hoarse whisper, but Eric heard it.

And he obeyed.

Five

Going Shopping

Thrown back by the sudden blast, Neal rolled away from the palace.

By the time he stopped, the boy he thought was Eric was gone.

"Was that really him?" Neal asked himself. "No way. That wasn't Eric. Eric would never blast me. It couldn't be him."

The sudden howling of wingwolves reminded Neal to hurry back to his friends. He dusted himself off, felt around, and found the carpet. Covering himself completely, he made his way to the stable and entered right under the noses of Captain Talon and his crew.

Inside Neal found his friends gathered around the magic mirror. "Guys," he said, "you totally won't believe who I saw —"

"Hush," Pasha whispered. "The magic mirror. It's not good. Eric . . ."

The mirror showed Galen, Max, and Relna in the royal bedchamber. On the bed beside them lay Eric, his face now no more than a ghostly shadow on the pillow.

"Every moment that passes, Eric grows more pale, less here," Galen said into the mirror. "The ice dagger's curse is drawing him away bit by bit, taking him somewhere —"

"That's exactly what I'm trying to tell you!" said Neal. "Eric is here!"

Keeah turned. "You saw Eric? Here?"

"At first he was so pale I almost *didn't* see him," said Neal. "When I *did* see him, he didn't know me. Then a dream came out of the palace, and Eric became more real, and he blasted my feet!"

"My worst fear," said Galen from the mirror. "The curse has released Eric's dark side. As he fades away from here, he reappears in Samarindo —"

"Hold on!" said Pasha. "Another dream!"

But as the children braced themselves amid the quivering walls of the stable, they were stunned to see what happened on the other side of the mirror.

As if the dream rippling through Samarindo traveled halfway across the world, the royal bedchamber wobbled and twisted for an instant, leaving Eric paler than ever.

"That's it!" said Keeah. "Whoever stole the Dream Crown is bringing Eric here —"

"The more the merrier!" said a voice.

At that moment, the stable vanished completely, and the kids found themselves standing in a courtyard of gray stone. There before them was Captain Talon with his band of growling wingwolves.

"Your hiding place is now our finding place," he said. "Shall we get 'em, boys?"

"Get 'em!" the wolves agreed.

With fierce swiftness, the wingwolves swooped down at the friends.

"Oh, no, you don't!" shouted Keeah.

Blam! Blam! She blasted the air with sparks, and the wingwolves scattered.

"The river's that way!" said Neal, tossing the carpet up into the air. "Everyone underneath, now!"

The friends huddled together and

disappeared from sight as the carpet fell over them.

"Where'd they go?" snarled Talon. "Old Red Eyes will be mad if we lose 'em! Spread out, boys!"

As the wolves flew around, frantically looking for them, the four friends made their way quietly from street to street.

"Did you hear Captain Talon?" asked Pasha. "Old Red Eyes? He's the one in the palace!"

Keeah peered up at the gigantic palace. The last dream had sapped its color entirely. It loomed over them, big and black. A long, curved tower had appeared on its summit.

"As soon as we find the cure," said Keeah, "we're going in there after Eric. That's got to be the only way to free him."

The four friends hugged the riverbank and soon found themselves in a warren of dark streets, winding alleys, and dead ends.

"You know, Samarindo gets spookier with every dream," said Julie.

"No kidding," said Neal. "Okay, if I were a Silver Dome, where would I be?"

"If only Isha were here to tell us which way to go," said Pasha. "Isha? Come back —"

Tweeeeeet!

The friends turned, and there was the green bird, perched on the handle of a little wooden cart that stood in the center of the narrow street.

"Isha! You darling bird!" cried Julie.

Sitting atop the cart next to Isha was a silver bowl upon whose sides were etched strange signs and characters.

Keeah picked up the bowl, turning it to try to read the characters. "I don't know the language. Eric might — oww!"

The bowl's sharp edges scratched Keeah's finger, and she dropped the bowl.

It landed upside down.

The children gasped — for upside down, the silver bowl looked like something else.

"The Silver Dome!" said Neal.

"Customers!" said a gray-haired old woman in a drab red cloak, appearing suddenly behind the cart.

Keeah jumped. "Yes. We were told —"

"Can I interest you in a shirtless collar?" asked the woman. "How about a pair of short-sleeved boots? Perhaps an invisible jacket is what you're after?"

She pinched her fingers together and lifted what looked like nothing.

"How do you know when you're wearing an invisible jacket?" asked Julie.

"When you don't see it on you!" said

the old woman. "It is a priceless treasure. But for you, a mere eight kopecks!"

"Please," Keeah began. "We're here because a friend of ours is very ill. We were told —"

"To find a cure?" the woman said suddenly, folding the unseen jacket carefully and replacing it on the cart. "Let me see, a boy was struck by an ice dagger and now you want to prevent him from fading away?"

The children were dumbfounded.

"How did you know that?" asked Julie.

"I have ears all around the world!" the woman said with a cackle. "But listen! This curse is ancient and dark. The boy will soon fade from the light and reappear in darkness. He will be drawn away from the good in him until only evil remains. Once that happens, he will be lost."

"Not Eric," said Pasha.

"What about the cure? There must be some hope," said Julie.

"Only one hope," said the woman. "Only one."

"What is it?" asked Keeah.

"Our true selves appear in dreams," the old woman said. "To save the boy, you must enter his dream before he is lost completely."

"How do we enter his dream?" asked Neal.

The old woman cackled again. "Like you enter anything else. First, you must come properly dressed. Second, you must pay the price of admission."

Keeah frowned. "What does that mean?"

The old woman tapped the upside-down bowl. "We'll start simple. You discovered that the opposite of a silver bowl is a silver dome. What's the opposite of a silver dome?"

"A silver bowl?" said Julie.

Keeah turned the dome over. Clinging to the inside was a silver necklace the color of moonlight. From it hung a single ruby in the shape of a drop of blood.

Keeah looked at her finger. The scratch was as red as the ruby. "That necklace wasn't there before. How did you —"

"Wear it when you see your friend again, Keeah," the woman said.

The princess blinked. "You know my name?"

"Oops, I've said too much!" the woman said. "Wear that to enter Eric's dream!"

"You know Eric's name, too?" said Neal.

"Oh, boy. I'm out of here!" said the woman, and she vanished from sight.

Julie gasped. "Keeah, look! Your neck!"

The ruby necklace was no longer in the bowl. Instead, it was dangling from Keeah's neck.

Pasha studied the necklace. "So if you are now properly dressed, all that remains to enter Eric's dream is to pay the price of admission, whatever that means. I suggest that if he is in the palace, that's where we must go —"

Oooo-ooo! A terrifying howl echoed in the air. Looking up, the children saw a dozen golden wings circling the palace.

"Fire dragons!" said Pasha. "Hide!"

But before the friends could escape, hands thrust out of the shadows and grabbed them.

Six

So Many Wings

The instant the palace doors slammed behind Eric, torches flared on either side of a narrow passage hewn out of gray stone.

Eric smelled smoke, but it wasn't coming from the torches. It was drifting down the passage from the dusky distance.

Acting on instinct, he followed the smell down the passage, through twists and turns, until he came to a large stone room. The room was nearly empty except for a wood fire roaring in a pit hollowed out of the floor.

Eric watched the smoke drift up from the pit and take the shape of . . . of . . . what?

The shape of a wing.

Just like the shadow on the ground.

As Eric watched, one, two, three, four wings appeared. Then a massive, horned head, a body, and steely claws.

On its head was a crown of brilliant gold, sparkling with emeralds.

Soon the smoke grew into the monstrous shape of a dragon with frightening red eyes.

"So," the dragon said. "You came."

"I guess so," said Eric. "Where am I?"

"Perhaps you are home," said the dragon.

Eric wasn't sure about that. He tried to

think back, but he couldn't actually remember his home, so he said nothing.

"Does your wound hurt?" asked the dragon.

Eric touched his shoulder. "Not so much."

The dragon smiled. "I didn't think so. It put you into a dream state, very like death. That is how we are able to meet here. How much do you remember of being wounded, Eric?"

"My memory's not so good," said Eric. "Is that my name? Eric?"

A snort like an icy breeze came from the smoky dragon. "Not for long. But you remember me, don't you, Eric? We're old friends."

Eric peered closely at the smoky image. It was strange, but somehow he did remember the creature. He had seen the four big wings before, and the glittering eyes.

The dragon had an odd name.

It came to him.

"Gethwing?" he said.

"Very good," said the dragon, growing more substantial. He flexed his wings.

"But aren't you in the Underworld?" Eric asked, wondering how he knew that.

The dragon twisted his mouth in a way that Eric knew was supposed to be a smile. "Even from the Underworld, I was able to call in some favors. The wing-wolves stole this crown for me. The fire dragons came to protect me. Since Emperor Ko is gone, I was able to use the crown to take over his curse. Samarindo is an amazing place. It makes dreams come true. And speaking of dreams coming true, you remember the prophecy, don't you?"

Eric thought and thought. His mind felt as smoky as the room. It was a fog of shapes and words he couldn't quite make out.

"The ice dagger?" said Gethwing.

Eric's heart skipped. He touched his shoulder. "That's right. An ice dagger struck me."

"Because of the prophecy," said the dragon.

That didn't sound right. "No," said Eric. "It was an accident. I tried to save . . . someone."

With each word that Eric spoke, the dragon grew more whole, more real, less ghostly.

"Whether or not you were the target, you were struck, and here you are," said Gethwing. "In a way, you *did* fulfill the prophecy. You are special, you know. You are powerful. One of the most powerful of all the wizards."

"No," said Eric. "How am I special?"

The dragon stared at him. "Zara."

"Ahh . . ." Eric winced. A pain went through his wound, sending shivers through his shoulders, his chest, his heart.

"The mother of wizards is called . . . Zara," said the dragon.

Again Eric's heart ached. "Stop!"

"I did that just to show you. You are special in a way few others are," said Gethwing. "I know that because I think that the prophecy is . . . well . . . never mind. All in due time."

"But wait," said Eric. "Tell me everything. I really can't remember too much. My brain feels . . . empty."

"Empty?" said Gethwing. "Good. Let's fill it up!" The smoky moon dragon fluttered his wings and grew larger still, rising to the ceiling. When he did, smoke drifted from the fire into other shapes.

"What's happening?" Eric asked.

Gethwing's terrible jaws twisted into a smile again. "Look, and tell me who you see."

Eric saw faces in the smoke. The girl wearing the blue tunic and the gold crown. The floating head that had called to him. A tall man with a beard. An odd spider with a mass of unruly orange hair. A purple, pillow-shaped creature.

The more Eric studied the faces, the less he seemed to know them.

"Who are these people?" asked Eric.

"What did you say?" Gethwing asked.

"Who are these people?" he asked.

"Excuse me?"

"WHO ARE THEY?" shouted Eric.

The moon dragon flapped his wings, and the smoky faces vanished. "No one," he said. "Not anymore. And the dagger's curse has done its work. Now look at . . . *this*!"

With a wave of the dragon's claw, the smoke formed a vast battalion of ships crossing a rough sea. Overhead flew a force of thousands of fire dragons, black-winged serpents, and scaly airborne lizards.

"Is this a dream?" asked Eric.

"One that can come true," said the dragon. "If you join me . . . Prince Ungast!"

"Prince Ungast?" said Eric. "Who's he?"

"He's . . . you!" said Gethwing.

Prince Ungast. The name sounded strange and odd. But in a way it also sounded right to Eric. Ungast. It sounded natural. Ungast. His name.

"I like it," said Eric. "When do I get all those ships and serpents and stuff?"

"First, you have to dress the part," said Gethwing. "How would you like a cloak? And some high boots? A pair of jeweled gloves?"

The dragon whispered, and two wing-wolves entered the chamber. They carried a black cloak studded with silver moons, and boots and gloves to match.

Eric pulled the heavy cloak over his shoulders. He felt as if his wound would smart under the weight of the cloak, but there was no pain. He donned the gloves, stepped one by one into the black boots, and stood tall.

Suddenly, his fingertips tingled.

Eric remembered sprinkling silvery sparks at someone recently, but the sparks flying from him now were jet black. As they struck the floor, they jangled like raucous bells.

"Try them," said the dragon.

Eric aimed his hands and blasted great holes into the walls, showering the two wingwolves with dust. They ran squealing from the room.

Eric laughed. "The sparks are cool. But . . . I don't think I need these any- more." He took off his glasses and dropped them to the floor.

"That's better," he said. "I see perfectly."

"It's a deal, then," said Gethwing, becoming more solid by the moment. "Agreed?"

Eric felt his gloved hand move through the smoky air to Gethwing. The dragon raised the gnarled claw of his left hand.

Eric touched the moon dragon's claw.

The moment he did, the smoke hard- ened into Gethwing's monstrous shape, and the dragon became whole. With a swift flash of his wings, Gethwing extin- guished the fire, the smoke vanished, and the moon dragon was completely present in the room. He was his old self again — evil, powerful, and cunning.

"You see, Prince Ungast," he said, "you really are powerful. With just a touch of your hand, you've helped me return to my world. Now let's see about getting you the things you want."

Gethwing strode toward a dark doorway at the rear of the chamber. "This world of Droon — and the world above it — will soon belong to us. But first I have a mission for you. Some troublemakers have entered our city. I want you to eliminate them."

"Can I use my sparks?" Eric said with a frosty smile. "My fingertips are itchy."

"Make them sizzle, Prince Ungast!" said the dragon. "And to help, meet . . . Gondra!"

Seven

The Dream Crown

The hands that shot out from the shadows dragged Neal to the ground. By his hair.

"Hey!" he screamed.

"Sarla! Looma! Leave that boy alone — and hush!" squeaked a little man in yellow robes. "Those fire dragons will hear you!"

"Yes, Father," replied the giggle twins.

They all scrambled deeper into the

shadows as a host of golden dragons swept overhead.

"Forgive my daughters," whispered the little man. "They're not used to such hair in Samarindo. I am Boola. Until last Tuesday I was the duke of Samarindo."

"You're still Daddy to us," said Looma.

"Thank you, dear," said the duke.

The friends watched as the dragons circled over the streets one more time, then again, and finally flew on together.

"I don't like them," said Pasha.

"You haven't seen the largest," said Sarla. "He's known by the silly name of Gondra."

"Why is that silly?" asked Neal.

"G-o-n-d-r-a," said Looma, "are the same letters as d-r-a-g-o-n mixed up!"

"Tell us what happened," said Keeah. "We believe whoever stole your crown is behind what's happening to our friend."

"I only use my powerful Dream Crown on special occasions," Boola said. "Tuesday, a snotty wingwolf broke into the treasury and stole it. Now Samarindo's reputation as the official City of Dreams is kaput!"

Keeah peered out at the dark palace, where a second and third curved tower had appeared. The palace was starting to look like a dragon's head.

And all at once, she knew.

"Old Red Eyes?" she said. "Of course! I should have guessed! Gethwing! He can't resist dragon-shaped palaces."

"But he's supposed to be lost in the Underworld," said Neal.

"He must have gotten the wingwolves to help him steal the crown," Keeah said. "It helped him make his way back here."

Boola went pale. "Gethwing? Everyone knows him. He's ruthless! Oh, my poor City of Dreams has become a nightmare!"

"Our best friend is caught right in the middle of this nightmare. We need to save him," said Neal. "What can we do?"

Boola stroked his chin. "The truest way to find your way in a dream — even a bad one — is to be swept away by it. I can get us into the palace. From there —"

"We'll do the rest," said Keeah.

The duke nodded. "Then follow me!"

The friends hoisted the carpet over their heads, making them invisible once more. Quickly, they began to march through the streets.

Sarla and Looma held on to Neal's arms. "So we can keep an eye on you," Looma said.

"And off my hair!" said Neal.

Holding the weaver's carpet high, the four friends and three Samarindians wove through the streets. Though dreams came and went, Boola's steps did not hesitate.

"Look at this," said the duke with a snort. "Hazards everywhere. Rickety bridges, streets circling upon themselves and going nowhere, sudden canals, deep ponds. I don't care for Gethwing's dreams at all. Not at all."

When they reached the palace at last, it loomed larger than ever, a monstrous hulk of black stone in the shape of a dragon's head.

"Our poor home!" said Sarla.

Just as the little band set foot on the path leading to the gates, a cry echoed through the streets.

"Oh, no! Look!" cried Pasha.

Shapes moved overhead. Shapes of many wings flapping in unison. The sky filled with row upon row of golden dragons flying in formation over the city.

"The fire dragons are back!" said Neal.

"Gethwing's terrible dream is becoming more real by the second!" said Keeah. "We have to stop this —"

"Wait!" said Sarla. "Look there. The dragons brought their terrible leader!"

"Gondra!" cried Looma.

The children watched, dumbfounded, as the largest dragon they had ever seen moved slowly over the city.

Its great head turned this way and that, searching the dark streets below.

All at once, the children spied a tiny figure riding on Gondra's back.

He had a black cloak and black boots and scowled when he saw the children.

"Who is *that*?" said Keeah.

Pasha gasped. "Oh, no, no, no . . ."

For when Gondra banked low, the children saw the rider's face.

It was familiar to them.

"I think we just found Eric," said Neal.

The rider's eyes stared coldly at the children, as if he didn't know them.

Julie felt her heart skip a beat. "But what happened to him? He's not wearing glasses . . . his eyes . . . he's . . . different!"

"The Dream Crown!" said Boola. "Gethwing must have used it to capture your friend's mind!"

The dragon rider snarled at the children, then raised his black gloved hand. "Gondra, attack those troublemakers!"

Oooo-ooo! howled Gondra.

And the fire dragons coiled together in a single mass and dived at the little band.

Eight

Mirror, Mirror, in the Hand

Prince Ungast pulled Gondra's reins, and the fire dragon dived swiftly.

Blam! Blam! Black sparks streamed from the dark prince's gloved fingers and strafed the street below.

The friends scurried to safety under a low stone bridge. Keeah's fingers sparked.

"Do we really have to fight our friend?" asked Julie, gasping for breath.

The princess shook her head. "No. We

have to fight *for* our friend. If Gethwing has used Ko's curse and the Dream Crown to draw the evil side of Eric out, we have to help his good side battle it."

"But how?" asked Neal.

Keeah didn't know exactly how. But she couldn't forget the cure hanging around her neck. Nor could she forget the old woman's words about entering Eric's dream.

Pay the price of admission.

Pay the price.

She fired a blast into the sky, careful to aim at Gondra's tail and not near Eric.

Wha-boom-boom! The fire dragon squealed and coiled away. As one, the flock of orange-scaled dragons shrieked and swept back into the sky after it.

"Ooooh, nice!" yelled Looma.

"That was good!" cried Sarla.

"We should split up," Keeah told Boola and his daughters. "If Gethwing is in the palace, you may still have a chance to steal back the crown. We'll give you cover while you run to the palace."

"We'll meet you inside later," said Neal.

"Really? When?" said Sarla, her fingers reaching for Neal's hair.

"Just . . . later!" said Neal, pulling away.

Boola nodded. "We'll do it. My head itches for that crown to sit back where it belongs. While you battle the dragons, I'll find a way to get my crown back. Girls?"

"We're with you, Daddy!" said Looma.

As the yellow-robed duke and his daughters zigzagged to the palace gates, Keeah blasted at the sky to confuse the dragons and give cover to her new friends.

Blam! Blam! The sky lit up with blasts.

"Eric!" called Julie as the dragon swooped low. "Don't you know us?"

"Who is Eric?" snarled the boy on Gondra's back. "I am Prince Ungast!" He raised his hands and hurled a blast of black fire at his friends.

Ka-blam!

"Eric!" called Neal. "This is only Gethwing's dream, his horrible dream —"

"A dream in which I'm the star!" said Ungast coldly. "How do you like my role so far? Now give up or pay the price!"

He sent stinging blasts of sparks at the street. *Boom! Boom!*

"Pay the price?" said Keeah. As she looked into Eric's stony face, she suddenly understood what the old woman meant.

"To enter Eric's dream, I have to pay the price!" she cried. "The ultimate price! The only way is to battle him. To be wounded —"

"Are you kidding?" said Julie. "You're going to fight him? For real?"

"What if he hurts you?" asked Neal.

Keeah touched the ruby necklace. "I think that's the point. I have to be wounded as he was —"

"No!" cried Julie. "You can't!"

"Keeah!" said Pasha. "Please don't!"

"Pasha, I need the carpet," said Keeah calmly. "It's the only way. I'll bring Eric back to us, or . . . or . . ."

She didn't dare say what she was thinking. But she didn't have to. Reluctantly, Pasha slipped the carpet from his pocket and gave it to her.

Keeah laid it flat on the ground, sat on it, and gave the front fringes a tug. *Whooosh!* She swept far up into the evening sky and straight for Eric and the giant fire dragon.

As she banked high over the palace, she gazed at the desert outside the city. Ranged on the dunes were hundreds of war tents, each one lit by a flaming torch.

"Gethwing's nightmare!" Keeah said to

herself. More determined than ever, she turned sharply and flew at Gondra's rider.

"Face me, will you?" Ungast yelled, his face twisted in anger. He dug his heels into the dragon's sides. "Then prepare to fall!" His fingertips exploded with black sparks.

Keeah's carpet reeled from the blasts. She yanked it to the left and swooped high over the fire dragon.

But the beast was as nimble as a sparrow. Ungast tugged the reins and it corkscrewed in the air, circling around behind the princess.

Keeah knew that the time had come. She was afraid, but she had put it off long enough, and now there was no escape.

Closing her eyes to speak a loving word to her faraway parents, she set her carpet on a collision course with Gondra.

"This — is — it!" Ungast aimed a huge blast of black sparks at the princess.

Wha-blammm! The blast struck Keeah's necklace like an arrow hitting its target.

Keeah screamed. As she fell, she knew it was the most powerful blow she'd ever received. She hurtled head over heels from the carpet.

"Oh, dear, no!" cried Pasha, clutching Julie and shutting his eyes, unable to look.

Pressing her miniature magic mirror to herself, Keeah fell, fell, fell to the city below.

Julie and Neal raced to try to catch Keeah before she struck the ground. But as they drew close, they saw her fade before their eyes until she vanished into her own magic mirror.

Her friends were dumbstruck.

"She's gone into Eric's dream!" cried Pasha, his lips trembling. "Poor Keeah!"

Gondra coiled straight up into the sky, while Prince Ungast howled at the top of his lungs, "Yahooooo!"

Nine

Adventures in Dreamland

Keeah fell for a long time — or maybe it was a short time. She couldn't tell. But when she opened her eyes, she was in the royal bedchamber in Jaffa City. It was evening. Candles flickered on tables beside the bed.

The little mirror was still in her hand.

The room was nearly empty. Queen Relna sat alone at Eric's bedside. Lord Sparr sat in the shadowy corner, as before. Galen and Max were likely in the wizard's tower and her father, the king, on his way to faraway Mikos.

"Mother?" Keeah said. "Mother —"

But the queen remained huddled over the bed as if she hadn't heard her daughter.

"Sparr?" Keeah said, turning to the corner.

No answer from the sorcerer.

"They don't hear me or see me," she said to herself. "So . . . it worked. The necklace has brought me . . . into the dreamworld."

All at once, her mother cried aloud, stood, and turned away from the bedside.

Keeah looked down and gasped. "No!"

The blankets lay flat. The pillow showed the indentation of a head, but no head was there. Eric had faded completely.

"No!" Keeah sobbed. "Eric! No!"

"Why is everyone crying?" said a voice from the corner of the room.

Keeah turned. "Who's there?"

Someone stepped from the dusky shadows, a figure more of mist than of flesh and blood.

"Can you see me?" he asked.

Keeah gasped. "Eric? Eric! It's you!" She tried to wrap her arms around him, but couldn't. Her hands went through him easily. She shuddered and tried not to show her fear. "I can't believe it's you!"

"I've been trying to talk to your mom," he said, practically crying, "but she doesn't hear me. I feel as if I died or something —"

"No," she said, trembling.

"Well, I look on the bed and I'm not there," said Eric, "and I'm barely even *here*. I feel like a ghost. What's happening to me?"

For a moment, Keeah wondered what

to say, then decided that she simply had to tell him, and quickly.

"The curse of the ice dagger put you into a deep sleep," she explained. "Then Gethwing . . . Gethwing used the power of dreams to draw you halfway across the world. I've seen you there."

"You've seen me?" he asked. "Where?"

"The dream city of Samarindo," she said.

Eric nodded when he heard the name. "Samarindo. I remember. So I'm still alive?"

"There's some not-so-good news," Keeah said. "Gethwing has unlocked your evil side. Eric, you're bad."

Eric looked surprised. "I have an evil side?"

"You call yourself Prince Ungast," she said.

"Ungast? That's so creepy," said Eric. "It's like what happened to you. Your evil twin called herself Neffu. All wizards go through a trial like this, don't they?"

Keeah nodded. "I remember Neffu every day of my life."

"He won't win, will he?" asked Eric. "Ungast won't win against me, will he?"

Looking at Eric's ghostly form, Keeah was unsure how to answer. "I hope not. He wears a heavy black cloak. His face is hard. And your silver sparks? Well, they're black now. And believe me, they hurt."

Eric's eyes widened. "Did I blast . . . you?"

Keeah touched the ruby stone on her necklace and recalled the fierce blow. "A little. But if you hadn't wounded me, I wouldn't be here now. Look, along with everything else, time is against us. We need to get you to Samarindo now, or . . . well, we just need to go."

Eric understood. "How do we get there?"

"The same way your other self did," she said. "Through the magic mirror. Ready?"

"I'm ready," said Eric.

Keeah stepped toward Galen's magic mirror, then turned to the silent figure on the stool. "Lord Sparr, you said you wouldn't abandon Eric. I wish you could come with us now." She placed her hand on his shoulder. "Thanks for Isha —"

Under the pressure of her fingers, however, the sorcerer's tattered cloak collapsed to the floor.

There was nothing underneath!

"Wait, Sparr is a ghost, too?" asked Eric.

Keeah gasped. "But —"

She suddenly knew why the old woman

in Samarindo had known her name. And Eric's.

"Sparr didn't abandon you!" Keeah cried. "He never abandoned you. He's been in Samarindo the whole time, and I know exactly where to find him! Let's go!"

The two friends jumped through the mirror. An instant later, they were back on the streets of the dream city.

But even in that short time, things had changed. Spreading out for miles beyond the dragon palace were more war tents than ever. They extended as far as the eye could see. Next to the tents were thousands of wingwolves and fire dragons, all standing at attention.

"Gethwing's dream army!" Keeah said. "Ungast will lead them against Droon."

"I will? I mean, he will?" said Eric.

"Not if we win *this* battle first," said Keeah. "We need to battle Ungast, and we need some help, the best help there is. Hurry. Look for a strange little cart!"

They rushed through the streets as quickly as they could until, all at once — *tweeeeeet!*

A little green bird swept over their heads.

"Isha!" gasped Keeah. "Lead us!"

The little bird led the two friends in and out of alleys and right under a wooden bridge to where the little cart stood alone.

"Sparr!" Keeah called out as they approached. "Sparr. I know it's you!"

A face popped up from behind the cart. This time, it was Sparr's familiar face. He was dressed in the old woman's drab red cloak. He leaned on his rusty saber. He was old and blind. But he was smiling.

"So it *was* you!" said Keeah.

"Look who the clever one is," said Sparr.

"You said you'd never abandon Eric," said Keeah. "And you're a sorcerer of your word."

"I am old and blind, and yet I sensed Gethwing trying to return from the Underworld," said Sparr. "I knew he might take advantage of Eric's curse to make his own dreams come true. Pretending to take up the vigil in the royal bedchamber, I actually came here and concocted a magic cure. Keeah, you played your part well."

"Thank you," she said.

"And thanks for helping me," Eric said.

Sparr's face turned grim. "Don't thank me yet. You must defeat Prince Ungast — or be defeated by him. There is no room for both of you. Thanks to Gethwing, the curse, and the Dream Crown, Ungast is already far more powerful than you!"

Eric looked at his ghostly hands. "So how can I fight him? I'm barely here."

"That may work to your advantage," said Sparr. "I am old, but I still know a thing or two about battling enemies. I'll show you moves you can use. Watch and learn!"

The sorcerer handed Eric his rusty saber. "It won't take long for Ungast to sense you are here," he said. "We must hurry. Keeah, tell me when the moon is at its height."

"I will," she said.

"Then — on guard!" said Sparr.

For the next hour, the old sorcerer taught Eric one move after another.

"Wake up! Look there!" he shouted, spinning on his heels. "Sense the position of your enemies. They give off an aura of evil. Imagine someone behind you. Be quick about it, that person is you! Let Ungast tire himself fighting a ghost. But remember, with every success, you become

more visible *and* more vulnerable. Use the boy's cloak against him. Trip him up. Make him so angry, he makes a mistake. Use that mistake to defeat him!"

Clack! Clonk! Using his hands, Sparr parried Eric's blows. The more he instructed Eric, the more tired the boy became. Eric turned more visible, then less visible. He jabbed quickly, but recovered slowly.

"Again!" Sparr coaxed. "You are fighting for your life! Fake left! Spin! Duck! You know Ungast's moves. They are your own!"

"The moon is up," Keeah said finally.

"And so is our time," said the sorcerer, breathing hard. "Eric, ready or not, the hour has arrived. Magic is over now. Help is over now. Keep the saber. The rest is up to you."

Sparr laid his hands upon Keeah and Eric. They bowed their heads in thanks.

A moment later, the red cloak collapsed. It was empty.

Looking into her mirror, Keeah saw the figure in the corner begin to rock again.

"He did as much as he could," she said.

Holding Sparr's saber, which grew heavier by the moment, Eric nodded. "It's up to me."

"Hey, Eric! Is that you?" called a familiar voice. "Is that really the good you?"

It was Neal. He was rushing down the street to his friend. "It *is* you! Yay, Eric!"

Julie and Pasha were right behind him.

Eric smiled to see his friends. But his time had already run out.

There came a great flapping of wings, but it was not Gondra the fire dragon this time.

It was Gethwing himself.

His four massive wings thundered in a storm of dust as he dropped from the sky.

Riding on his back was Prince Ungast.

"What a surprise!" said Ungast, jumping to the ground and adjusting his collar. "Is it my birthday or something?"

"The opposite maybe," Eric said.

"And he's funny, too," Ungast snarled.

"You won't be laughing long," said Neal.

The moon dragon stretched his wings to the sky. "Perhaps not," said Gethwing, "but *I* will be. Wingwolves?"

"Let her go, boys!" called Captain Talon.

A heavy net of chains dropped right over Keeah, Neal, Julie, and Pasha. It flattened them to the ground and trapped them helplessly beneath it.

"My idea of a good time!" said Gethwing.

Ungast sneered as he slowly circled around Eric. "Why, there's barely any of you left to fight. I won't even break a sweat!"

Eric felt sure he would fail. He bit his lip to keep from fainting. "Don't be so sure," he said. "I know what to do with this blade. A friend gave it to me. Oh, sorry. Did I say 'friend'? Friends are something you don't know anything about —"

Ungast's smile dropped from his face. "I don't care about your saber or your friends. Let's see what *you're* made of. Not much, I bet!" He tossed his cloak back and thrust his hand high.

Voooomp! A sword of shimmering black steel rose from his jeweled glove.

"Blade to blade, little boy, let's see who's got the stuff!"

A Special Boy

Flang! Clomp! Bam!

As everyone watched, mesmerized, Eric managed to duck and dodge the first of Ungast's thrusts. He spun around on his heels as Sparr had taught him. He chopped and hacked with all his strength.

But it was clear he couldn't keep it up. Ungast was far stronger and faster.

Finally, Ungast leveled a blow against

...de out of his

"Did I win

...ish him —"

...twisting herself
...hrough the iron
chai... ...trated blasts. *Blam!*
Blam!... ...ers in a flash.

"Neal, give the wolves a bath!" said Pasha.

Neal laughed. "Great idea!"

"What? No. No!" cried Captain Talon. "We hate water —"

Unwrapping his turban, Neal whipped the cloth through the air. It became a wave of water that doused and scattered Captain Talon and his shrieking wingwolves.

"Eric, the carpet, quickly!" shouted Pasha. Even as the air flamed with sparks, Pasha flung the carpet across the ground, and Eric clambered onto it.

"No fair!" shouted Ungast. "Gethie!"

In a single move, the dark prince leaped onto the dragon's back and aimed blast after blast at Eric. *Blam! Blam!*

Eric dipped and swooped, trying to escape. The carpet was fast, but not as fast as Gethwing. The dragon followed close enough for Ungast to score a flaming hit.

Blam! Eric felt the sting of sparks on his wounded shoulder. He paled even more.

"Ungast gains power with every blast," cried Julie. "We need to help Eric!"

"I'm on it!" said Keeah. She conjured up fireballs and hurled them at Gethwing. The dragon howled in surprise.

Eric turned the carpet abruptly around and flew it straight at Gethwing. *Whump!* He rammed him right between the wings.

In anger, Gethwing thrust out his claws

and caught Eric's carpet with a talon. The carpet ripped. Eric clutched the air and caught the hem of Ungast's cloak. The two enemies screamed and dropped twenty feet onto the streets below.

Dazed, Ungast struggled to his feet. He looked for Eric and saw him pulling himself up from the ground. He raised his gleaming sword. "Now — to end it!"

Then came a shriek from above. As Gethwing circled behind the black palace, one of Keeah's fireballs sizzled at him.

"Enough of you!" the princess shouted.

The moon dragon batted the fireball away with his giant tail. But the tip of his tail struck the tallest horn of the palace with a fierce impact, and Gethwing faltered.

Ungast raged against Eric. "Enough of *you*!"

Eric remembered what Sparr had taught him and faked left, then twirled to his right, sticking his foot out. Ungast slid past him and tumbled flat on his face.

Ungast groaned and went still.

Eric fell to his knees. "I win! I win —"

WHOOOOM!

The impact of Gethwing's tail sent black stones flying everywhere, knocking the Dream Crown from his forehead and tangling his wings. He crashed into the tower, and the entire palace began to crumble.

Julie screamed. "Eric — watch out!"

Exhausted, Eric pushed his glasses up his nose and saw Duke Boola and his daughters escaping the palace. He tried to get to his feet but could not.

With a tremendous crash, the entire palace — and Gethwing himself — collapsed in a rush of tumbling stones and showering dust.

Directly onto Eric and Prince Ungast.

"No!" screamed Keeah. "Eric!"

The air thundered, and the ground quaked for what seemed like an eternity.

Finally, all was still once more.

Out of the debris came a flutter of tiny wings. Isha swooped around the wreckage over and over until she hovered over a single spot.

"There!" cried Pasha. "Dig there!"

Not waiting for the dust to clear, everyone climbed into the rubble and began digging.

"Eric!" Julie called. "Eric, can you hear us?"

"Where are you? Answer us!" yelled Neal, tossing smoking chunks of black stone behind him. "Eric —"

"Hush!" said Keeah, holding up her hand. "I hear something!"

The friends went silent.

Tap . . . tap . . .

Sounds of life came from deep under the wreckage. The children listened.

"Help . . . me . . ."

"Dig!" cried Keeah.

With all their strength, the friends picked away at the stones. Keeah blasted where she could, lifted stones gently when she could not.

When at last they could dig no farther, Julie yelled, "Eric! Are you there? *Eric?*"

Seconds passed. No sound.

Then a stone shifted. Dust stirred. Out of the rubble, a small figure emerged. It was a boy in rags. His brown hair stuck out every which way. He staggered from the wreckage, then fell to his knees. In his hand was a crumpled pair of glasses. He was no longer faded.

He was completely whole.

"Eric!" Keeah yelled. She ran and threw

her arms around him, overjoyed. "You made it! You made it!"

Neal, Julie, Pasha, and the twin princesses surrounded him.

"Eric!" Neal said, slapping his friend on the shoulder. "You're back!"

"I am?" Eric said, blinking his eyes. He managed a weak smile. "That was . . . amazing. Do . . . do you think he's really . . . gone?"

The children turned to the rubble. The remains of Ungast's cloak smoked among the rocks like a pile of burning leaves.

"I think so," Keeah said, wiping away her tears. "Gethwing, too. We thought we lost you, Eric. But you defeated him. You won!"

"Gethwing has been defeated," said Duke Boola. "The wingwolves have fled. The fire dragons have vanished. Our city

is restored. Samarindo rises from its ashes. Look!"

Below the ruins of Gethwing's palace lay the multicolored stones of Boola's original castle. Setting the dented crown on his head for the first time in days, the duke dreamed of colorful streets, and Gethwing's dark dream became the enchanted city again. The sun shone as at noon, and the streets filled with townspeople who set right to work clearing the rubble away.

At the same time — *whoosh!* — the rainbow stairs appeared, glittering in the blazing light of Boola's colorful palace.

"Such a dark day ends happily and full of light!" said Pasha. "Hooray!"

Keeah held on to Eric's hand. "Gethwing is defeated. I can't believe you did it. Eric, you won against your darkest self."

"Are you sure?" he said.

"I *am* sure," she said. "You are amazing."

"Could this mean that Droon will be at peace?" asked Pasha, gazing at the wreckage. "Ko and Gethwing, both gone? How wonderful it would be!"

Eric lifted his glasses and chuckled. The frames were bent like a pretzel.

"My glasses," he said.

"You can always get them fixed," said Julie.

"I can," said Eric. "But why would I want to?"

With that, the smile dropped from Eric's lips, his eyes went gray and cold, and he dropped the glasses to the ground. "I don't wear glasses."

"You'll need them at home," said Neal.

"Home?" said the boy, glaring at the children. "My home is in the Dark Lands."

"What?" said Julie. "Eric —"

"Eric doesn't live here anymore," he snapped. "My name is Ungast. Prince Ungast. Remember it. You'll be hearing the name a lot. I need to go now. Gethwing?"

The rubble exploded, and the air thundered with the flapping of giant wings. The moon dragon rose up from the remaining wreckage, larger and stronger than ever.

"Come, Gethie," Ungast said. "A new day awaits us. And a new Droon!"

"My dream come true!" said Gethwing.

"No!" cried Keeah. "No! No! No! No!" She fell to her knees. "Eric!"

"Oh, boo-hoo!" said Ungast.

With a laugh, the dark prince jumped onto Gethwing's back. He gave the dragon a sharp nudge, and together they flew up into the sky, winging their way straight to the heart of the Dark Lands.